Hello, you!

Oh, please don't look
inside the pages
of this book.

Turn around and quickly run ...

THIS BOOK BELONGS TO

SCHOOL OF MONSTERS

By Sally Rippin

PETE'S BIG FEET

Art by
Chris Kennett

Kane Miller
A DIVISION OF EDC PUBLISHING

Today the
monsters want
to run,

to see who is the fastest one.

The day they love
has just begun.

Monster Sports
Day in the sun!

But do you think
that Pete can **run**

with feet like his?
They are no fun!

WIGGLE

Last year he tried
to join a race.

He tumbled down,
fell on his
face.

TRIP

DONK!

BINK!

BANK!

Feet and legs
tied in a **ball**,

BONK!

he even cried
in front
of all.

Now poor old
Pete sits by
a **tree**,

to hide his
tears so they
won't see.

Even though the
monsters **call**,

Pete won't
risk another
fall.

Then suddenly
Pete hears a yell.

Jamie Lee is in the well!

SPLAT!

The well is muddy
and it's deep.

Pete stands up
and off he goes.

Soon Jamie
sees his great
big toes.

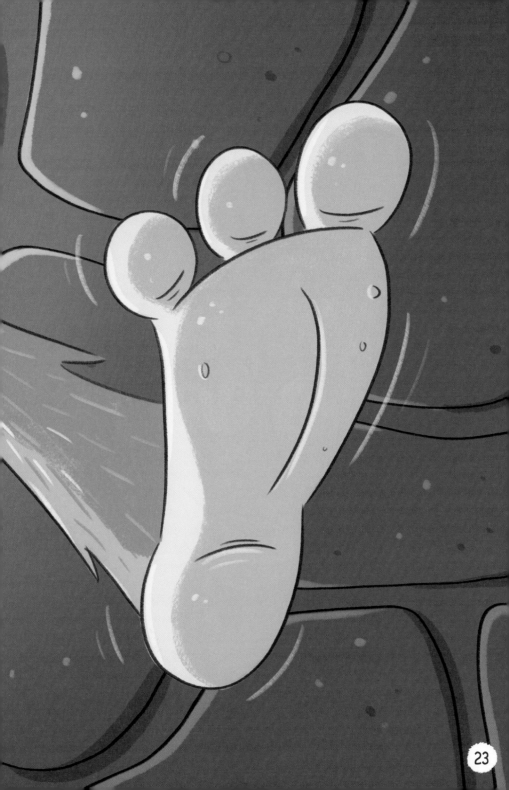

She reaches up.
Pete gives a shout.

"Grab my foot,
I'll pull you out!"

All the monsters yell,
"Oh yay!

Pete, your feet have saved the day!"

They pin a ribbon on his **chest**,

to tell the world that
Pete's the best.

So on the days
you can't fit in,

too big,
too small, or
just can't win ...

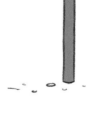

Remember Pete,
who saved the day,

and know that you will
find your **way**.

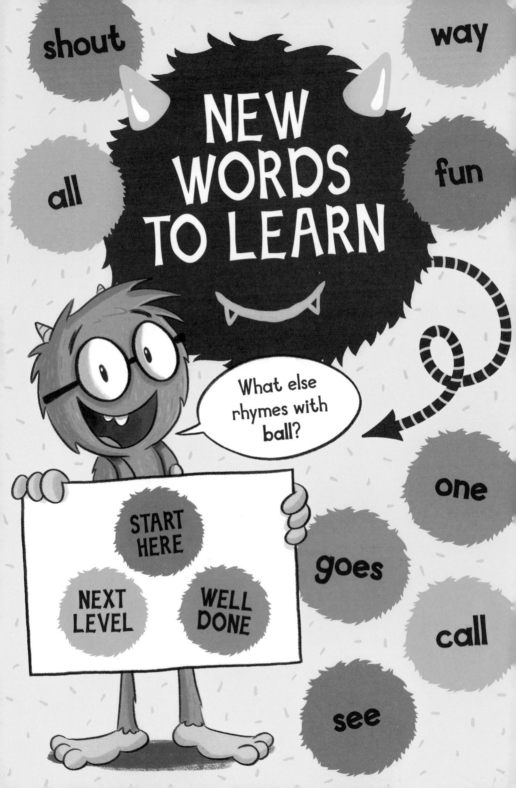

HOW TO USE THIS BOOK

for adults reading with children

Welcome to the School of Monsters!

Here are some tips for helping your child learn to read.

At first, your child will be happy just to listen to you read aloud. Reading to your child is a great way for them to associate books with enjoyment and love, as well as to become familiar with language. Talk to them about what is going on in the pictures and ask them questions about what they see. As you read aloud, follow the words with your finger from left to right.

Once your child has started to receive some basic reading instruction, you might like to point out the words in **bold**. Some of these will already be familiar from school. You can assist your child to decode the ones they don't know by sounding out the letters.

As your child's confidence increases, you might like to pause at each word in bold and let your child try to sound it out for themselves. They can then practice the words again using the list at the back of the book.

After some time, your child may feel ready to tackle the whole story themselves. Maybe they can make up their own monster stories, too!

Sally Rippin is one of Australia's best-selling and most-beloved children's authors. She has written over 50 books for children and young adults, and her mantel holds numerous awards for her writing. Best known for her *Billie B. Brown*, *Hey Jack!* and *Polly and Buster* series, Sally loves to write stories with heart, as well as characters that resonate with children, parents, and teachers alike.

HOW TO DRAW PETE

① Using a pencil, draw 2 circles for eyes and a big smiley mouth.

② Draw the frame of the glasses and a fuzzy circle for the head.

③ Draw a circle for the body with a line across the tummy. Then add 2 boxes for the shorts.

④ Add long tubes for the arms and legs.

5 Draw on the wristbands before adding the hands and feet. Add the straps too, while you're here. Use an eraser for overlapping lines.

6 Time for the extra details! Draw in his stripy tail, teeth, and eyebrows. Don't forget his HORNS on top!

Chris Kennett has been drawing ever since he could hold a pencil (or so his mom says). But professionally, Chris has been creating quirky characters for just over 20 years. He's best known for drawing weird and wonderful creatures from the *Star Wars* universe, but he also loves drawing cute and cuddly monsters – and he hopes you do too!

WELCOME
TO THE

SCHOOL OF MONSTERS

Have you read ALL the School of Monsters stories?

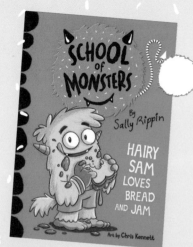

You shouldn't bring a pet to **school**.
But Mary's pet is super **cool!**

Sam makes a mess when he eats **Jam**.
Can he fix it? Yes, he **can!**

Today it's Sports Day in the sun.
But do you think that Pete can run?

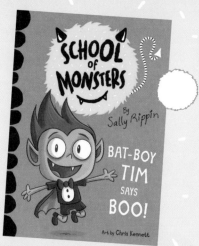

When Bat-Boy Tim comes out to play,
why do others run away?

Jamie Lee sure likes to eat!
Today she's got a special treat ...

Now that you've learned to read along with Sally Rippin's School of Monsters, meet her other friends!

Hey Jack!

Billie B. Brown

Down-to-earth, real-life stories for real-life kids!

Billie B. Brown is brave, brilliant and bold,
and she always has a creative way to save the day!

Jack has a big heart and an even bigger imagination.
He's Billie's best friend, and he'd love to be your friend, too!

Pete's Big Feet

First American Edition 2021
Kane Miller, A Division of EDC Publishing

First published in 2021 by Hardie Grant Children's Publishing
Ground Floor, Building 1, 658 Church Street Richmond,
Victoria 3121, Australia.

Library of Congress Control Number:
2020949017

ISBN: 978-1-68464-270-0

Printed in China through Asia Pacific Offset

10 9 8 7 6 5 4 3 2 1